This creature
book belongs to

_____

_____

_____

For my dad

and Tom, Chester, Blackie, Mitzi,
Bagpuss and Alfred

ORCHARD BOOKS

First published in Great Britain in 2006 by Orchard Books
This edition published in 2020 by The Watts Publishing Group

1 3 5 7 9 10 8 6 4 2

Text and illustrations © Sam Lloyd, 2006

The moral rights of the author-illustrator have been asserted.

A CIP catalogue record for this book is available from the British Library.

ISBN 978 1 40836 071 2

Printed and bound in China

MIX
Paper from
responsible sources
FSC
www.fsc.org   FSC® C104740

Orchard Books
An imprint of Hachette Children's Group
Part of The Watts Publishing Group Limited
Carmelite House
50 Victoria Embankment
London EC4Y 0DZ

An Hachette UK Company
www.hachette.co.uk

www.hachettechildrens.co.uk

Mr Pusskins

A PET'S TALE

Sam Lloyd

ORCHARD

This is the story of a little girl called Emily, and her dear cat, Mr Pusskins.

Emily adored Mr Pusskins.

Each morning, she would invent **fun games** for Mr Pusskins to play.

In the afternoons, she'd brush his long fur coat and tell him,

"Oh, Mr Pusskins, what a handsome boy you are! I do love you ever so much."

And each night, Emily would snuggle up in bed and read Mr Pusskins a special story.

But Mr Pusskins
never listened.

The girl's constant babbling,

"Blah~de~blah, blah, blah,"

bored his whiskers off.
He wanted more than this dull life.

He went places he **wasn't** meant to go;

did things he **wasn't** meant to do.

And even made friends with the **Pesky Cat Gang.**

Life without Emily was

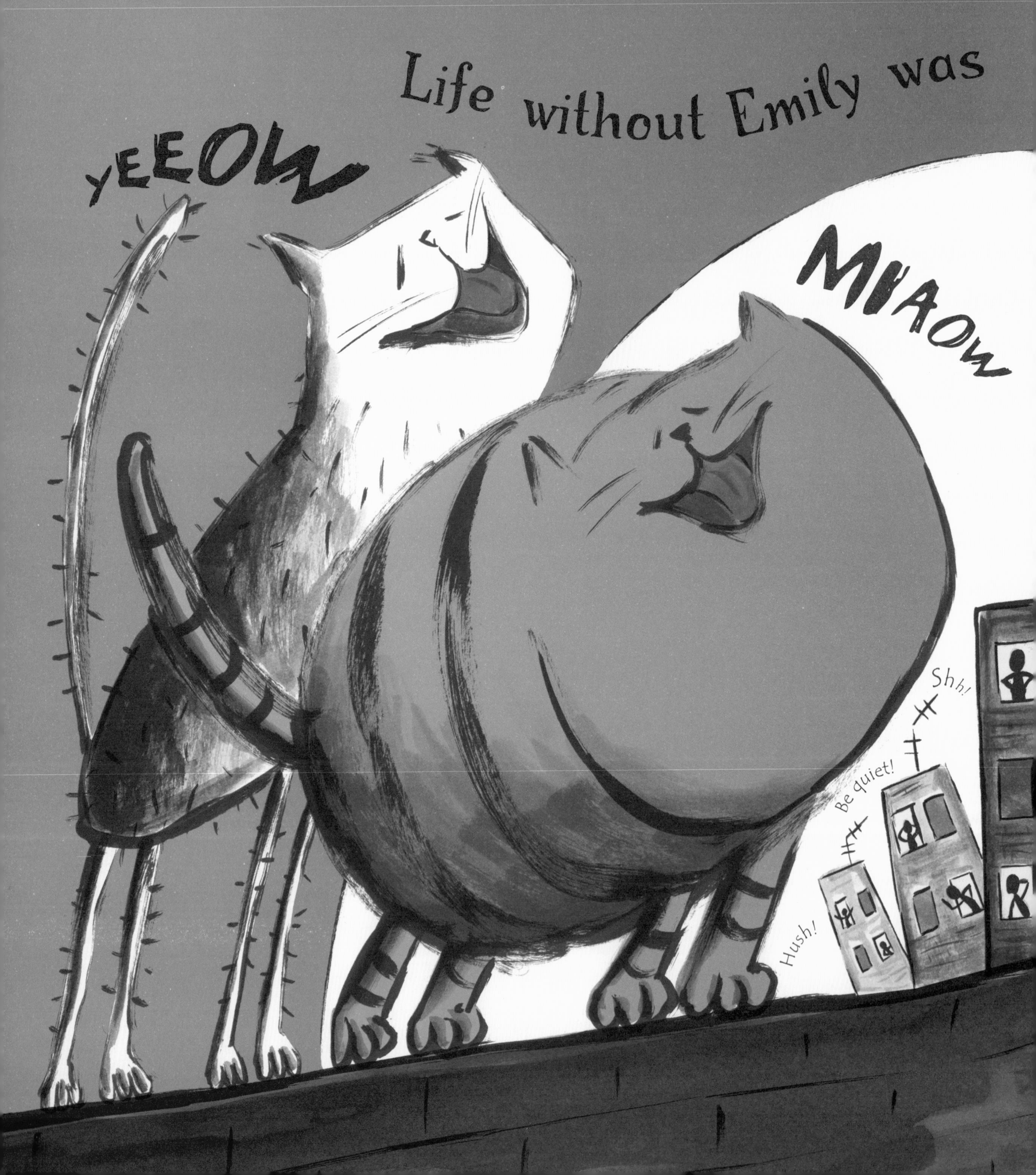

But time passed, and things **changed**.
The rain fell, and an icy wind blew.

The things Mr Pusskins wasn't supposed
to do weren't fun any more. And his new
friends weren't really very nice.

How lovely it would be to
have someone to brush his fur,
and tell him how much they loved him.

He felt all **alone**.

LOST:
Mr Pusskins
Phone: 693900

Then down the grey streets fluttered a tatty old poster. It was a picture of Mr Pusskins!

LOST:
Mr Pusskins
Phone: 693900

LOST:
Mr Pusskins
Phone: 693900

He stared at the photo.
What a bad-tempered cat he looked.
Emily had given him **everything**
a cat could ever dream of . . .

LOST
Mr Pusskins
Phone:

but he had
never been nice to her.

How
sorry
he felt.

Mr Pusskins found a phone box. He dialled the number from the poster, and waited anxiously.

Someone answered!

"Miaow," whimpered Mr Pusskins in a very sad little voice.

"Mr Pusskins! Is that you? Oh, thank goodness," said Emily. "Wait there, I'll come and get you!"

Mr Pusskins sat patiently.

Would Emily **find** him?

Did she still **love** him?

He waited
and **waited**.
But Emily didn't come.

Then, from over the mountains, he heard a car. Mr Pusskins' heart leapt!

It was Emily! His dear Emily was coming for him!

The car

got nearer

and nearer

and then . . . .

Br

. . . sped straight past.

"MIAAAAOOOOOOww!" wailed Mr Pusskins.
"Emily doesn't love me any more."

But then . . .

rrrrrm

. . . the car screeched to a halt and Emily jumped out. "Mr Pusskins! My **beautiful** Mr Pusskins!" she cried. "I didn't recognise you!"

Emily scooped up her dear cat.
At last, they were
together
again!

This is the end of the story of a little girl called Emily, and her dear cat, Mr Pusskins.

Mr Pusskins **adores** Emily.

Every evening, he cuddles her

and **purrs** gently while she reads to him.

And now both Emily and Mr Pusskins realise how lucky they are to have **each other.**